Storytime

First Tales
for Sharing

For Cecilia and Rufus — S. B.

For friendships and many shared tales — A. W.

Barefoot Books
2067 Massachusetts Ave
Cambridge, MA 02140

This book was typeset in Soupbone and Plantin
The illustrations were prepared in printed collaged papers with acrylic and printed backgrounds

Graphic design by Jemima Lumley, Bristol
Color separation by Bright Arts, Singapore
Printed and bound in China by South China Printing Co. Ltd

This book has been printed on 100% acid-free paper

1 3 5 7 9 8 6 4 2

Library of Congress Cataloging-in-Publication Data

Blackstone, Stella.
Storytime / written by Stella Blackstone ; illustrated by Anne Wilson.
p. cm.
Summary: Includes simplified retellings of seven traditional tales featuring animal characters.
ISBN 1-84148-345-1 (hardcover : alk. paper) 1. Tales. [1. Folklore. 2. Animals--Folklore.] I. Wilson,
Anne, 1974- ill. II. Title.

PZ8.1.B5822Ta 2005
398.2--dc22

2004029542

Storytime
First Tales
for Sharing

Told by Stella Blackstone

Illustrated by Anne Wilson

Barefoot Books
Celebrating Art and Story

CONTENTS

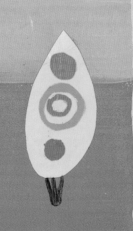

The Cock, the Mouse
and the Little Red Hen
6

The Gingerbread Man
20

The Ugly Duckling
32

Goldilocks and the Three Bears
46

The Timid Hare
56

The Three Little Pigs
68

Stone Soup
82

The Cock, the Mouse and the Little Red Hen

This is a story about a cock, a mouse, a little red hen and a crafty old fox.

The cock, the mouse and the little red hen all lived together in a red brick house. The little red hen was a hard worker. She kept the house as neat as a pin, she baked delicious pies and cakes and loaves of bread for everyone, and she always kept her scissors, needle and thread tucked in her apron, just in case something needed mending. I'm sorry to say that her companions were not as hardworking as she was. All the cock ever did was crow loudly every morning — "Cock-a-doodle-doo! Cock-a-doodle-doo!" And all the mouse did was sleep and eat and complain if he was too cold.

Not far away from the red brick house lived a crafty old fox and his family. One day, the crafty old fox could not find anything tasty in the woods to feed his wife and his four hungry fox cubs. "Hmmm," thought the crafty old fox. "If I could only catch the cock, the mouse and the little red hen, what a feast we would all have for our supper!"

So the crafty old fox made a cunning plan. He found a big, strong sack and the next day he got up very early. He took the sack and he walked all the way to the red brick house and knocked on the door.

The cock had only just woken up and was getting ready to come outside and sing "Cock-a-doodle-doo." He rubbed his eyes and opened the door, but before he could open his beak, the fox had grabbed him by the feet and stuffed him into the sack. The cock flapped and thrashed and squawked, and soon the mouse woke up in alarm. Quick as a flash, the crafty old fox grabbed him by the tail and swung him into the sack as well. Then he pounced on the little red hen and flung her in too.

"So far, so good," purred the fox, feeling rather pleased with himself. He tied a big knot in the top of the sack and set off for home. He had a long way to go, though, and the sack was heavy. The sun grew hotter and hotter, and soon the fox was very tired. "I'd better stop for a rest," he thought. So he settled down in the shade under a nearby tree and laid the sack down beside him. Then he fell asleep and started snoring.

Inside the sack, the cock and the mouse were trembling with fright. Only the little red hen remained calm. As soon as she heard the fox snoring, she knew that their chance had come. Without wasting a moment, she pulled out her scissors. Snip, snip, snip! Soon she had cut a neat hole in the sack. "Shhhhh!" she whispered to the cock and the mouse. Then each of them crept out, trying not to disturb the sleeping fox.

"Quick! Bring me some stones!" whispered the little red hen. The cock nearly jumped out of his feathers with surprise. "What's she bossing me around like this for?" he thought. Just then, the fox gave a big sigh and rolled over. The cock was nearly paralyzed with fear, and he realized that if he didn't change his ways and help the little red hen, he would become the fox family's dinner.

"Hurry up and help me!" he hissed at the mouse, and between them
they pushed three heavy stones over to the sack and rolled them in. "So
far, so good!" whispered the little red hen. Then she sewed up the sack
again, so neatly that it looked as good as new.

"Let's get out of here!" whispered the mouse, and the three friends ran
as fast as they could back to the red brick house.

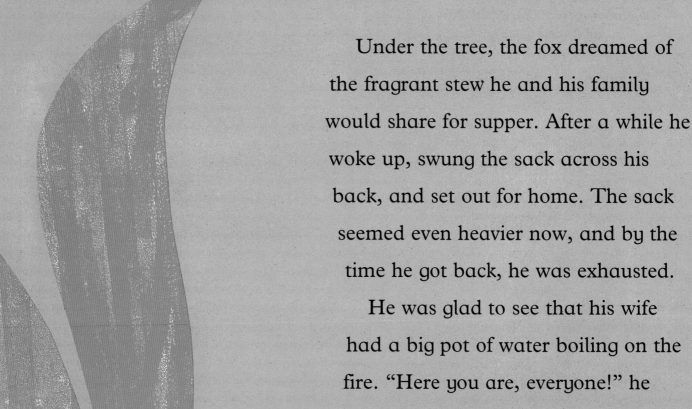

Under the tree, the fox dreamed of
the fragrant stew he and his family
would share for supper. After a while he
woke up, swung the sack across his
back, and set out for home. The sack
seemed even heavier now, and by the
time he got back, he was exhausted.
He was glad to see that his wife
had a big pot of water boiling on the
fire. "Here you are, everyone!" he
cried, and he tipped the sack right
into the water. Ouch! The heavy
stones sent boiling water splashing in
every direction, and all of the foxes were
scorched. The crafty old fox could not
believe it. He went slinking away to the
back of the den and curled up in a corner,
covering his face with his big, bushy tail.

The fox family did not have anything for supper that night. But the cock, the mouse and the little red hen baked a big apple pie to celebrate their escape, and everyone helped to make it. And from then on, the cock and the mouse took great care to help their clever and hardworking friend, the little red hen.

The Gingerbread Man

This is a story about a little old woman
and a gingerbread man.

The little old woman lived by herself in a cottage. One cold winter morning, she decided to do some baking. She mixed flour and butter and sugar and ginger to make her dough. Next she flattened the dough with a rolling pin and cut out a handsome gingerbread man. She gave him bright, black, currant eyes and a big, smiley mouth. Then she popped him onto a baking tray and slid him into the oven.

When the gingerbread man was ready, the old woman bent down to open the oven door. Mmmm! A delicious gingery smell wafted toward her as she slid out the baking tray. But no sooner had she done so, than the gingerbread man sat bolt upright on the tray and looked her right in the eye:

"You're not going to eat me!" he cried. "I'm running away!"

The old woman got such a shock that she dropped the baking tray on the kitchen floor. Before you could say "Snap!" the gingerbread man had raced out of the back door and down the back path.

"Come back here!" shouted the old woman, and she hitched up her skirts and raced after him.

But the gingerbread man just laughed and said:

"Run, run, as fast as you can! You can't catch me — I'm the gingerbread man!"

As he ran down the lane, the gingerbread man passed a farmer.

"Help me catch him!" cried the old woman. "Don't worry!" cried the farmer. "I'll stop him in his tracks!"

But the gingerbread man just laughed and said:

"Run, run, as fast as you can! You can't catch me — I'm the gingerbread man!"

25

At the bottom of the hill, the gingerbread man ran into the farmer's two children.

"Help us catch him!" cried the old woman and the farmer.

But the gingerbread man just laughed and said:

"Run, run, as fast as you can! You can't catch me — I'm the gingerbread man!"

The old woman and farmer and the farmer's children raced into the wood behind the gingerbread man. Soon they met a big brown bear.

"Stop him!" they cried.

But the gingerbread man just laughed and said:

"Run, run, as fast as you can! You can't catch me — I'm the gingerbread man!"

The gingerbread man ran deeper into the wood. He was far, far ahead of the old woman and the farmer and the farmer's children and the bear when he met a fox.

"You're a fast runner, aren't you?" said the fox.

"Yes, I am!" said the gingerbread man, and for the first time he stopped. "I ran faster than the old woman, and faster than the farmer, and faster than the farmer's children, and faster than the bear. I can run faster than you, too!"

"Could you say that a little louder?" asked the fox. "I couldn't quite hear you."

So the gingerbread man walked up to the fox and said:

"I ran faster than the old woman, and faster than the farmer, and faster than the farmer's children, and faster than the bear. I can run faster than you, too!"

The fox frowned. "If you could come a bit closer, perhaps I could hear you properly."

So the gingerbread man walked right up to the fox's nose and bellowed in his loudest voice:

"I ran faster than the old woman, and faster than the farmer, and faster than the farmer's children, and faster than the bear. I can run faster than you, too!"

"Can you, indeed?" said the fox. And before the gingerbread man could do anything else, SNIP, SNAP! the fox had swallowed him up in one gulp.

And that was the end of the gingerbread man.

The Ugly Duckling

This is a story about an ugly duckling
and his adventures.

One long, hot summer, a fine mother duck sat on her
nest, waiting for her eggs to hatch. At last she heard a
tap, tap, tapping sound, and all but one of her ducklings
pecked their way out of their shells. But one egg was
bigger than the others, and it did not hatch. So the
mother duck continued to sit on it, waiting and hoping.
A few days later, her patience was rewarded: crack,
crack, crack! The biggest egg broke open — but what a
strange sight came out of it!

This duckling was very big, and he was also very ugly.

The mother duck waddled down to the water with her ducklings and all of them jumped in behind her. As they bobbed happily up and down, she had a good look at her offspring. She noticed that the ugly one paddled beautifully, and held his long neck high and straight. "He may be big," she thought to herself, "and he may be rather strange-looking, but he is certainly an excellent swimmer."

It was soon time for the ducklings to be introduced to the rest of the farmyard. But when the family arrived, all of the other animals teased the big duckling. "You look so weird!" they sneered. Soon, the ugly duckling's life was miserable. The hens pecked him, the ducks snapped at him, and the girl who fed the poultry gave him a big kick every time she came to the farmyard.

One day, the ugly duckling could bear it no longer. He woke
up early, and flew quietly away, across the meadows, to the tall
reeds where the wild ducks made their home.

"Perhaps they will be kinder to me," he thought.

But the wild ducks were no better than the ones on the farm.

"What are you doing here?" they demanded. "You're
not one of us, you big, scraggly creature!"

The ugly duckling flew on. After a while he came to a
small, run-down cottage. "Perhaps I can stay here for a while,"
he thought, so he waddled up and pecked politely on the door.

Inside the cottage lived an old woman with her cat and her hen for company. She was quite pleased to find a duckling on her doorstep, even if he was rather an ugly one.

"Come in, come in," she said. "I'll look after you if you can give me some eggs."

So the ugly duckling lived at the old woman's cottage. But he could not lay any eggs, of course, and before long the old woman started to resent him. So did the cat and the hen. "You good-for-nothing!" jeered the cat. "I don't know why we bother with you. You're nothing to look at, and you can't even do anything useful, like catching mice or laying eggs."

The ugly duckling felt more and more lonely.
At the same time, he started to grow restless.
He knew he did not want to live in a cottage;
he wanted to be on the water. He wanted to be
able to float on the waves, and dive underneath
them for food. So he left the cottage and flew
far, far away to a beautiful lake.

Fall came. The leaves turned red and gold,
and the days were crisp and cold. One evening,
just before sunset, the ugly duckling saw three
beautiful swans floating on the lake not far
away from him. As he watched them, they
stretched out their wings and rose gracefully out
of the water. The ugly duckling cried out after
them, and his cry was quite unlike any sound
he had ever made. He watched them longingly
as they soared up into the evening sky,
and something stirred deep inside him,
something that he had never felt before.

The lake was quiet now, and the ugly duckling grew colder and colder as winter approached. The water at the edge of the lake froze. Then came a night wher the entire surface froze solid. The ugly duckling lay exhausted on the ice. Luckily he was spotted by a local farmer, who picked him up and carried him back to his farmhouse.

The farmer's wife laid the ugly duckling close to the kitchen fire and soon the warmth revived him. But he was very frightened by the farmer's

children. In fact, he was so scared that he flew into the milk pan and spilled it all. Then he knocked the butter churn over, and that knocked over the flour bin. Everyone shrieked with alarm, which frightened the ugly duckling even more. So he flew back out of the warm kitchen into the freezing cold. He grew thinner and thinner and hungrier and hungrier. Then, just when he thought that he could not last much longer, a warm wind blew again, and the leaves started to open on the apple trees. Spring had returned.

One sunny morning, the ugly duckling saw three swans sailing by. He was sure they would be nasty to him, but he decided that he would rather be pecked by these magnificent creatures than by hens or ducks. So he swam shyly toward them. "You can attack me if you like," he said, lowering his head. As he did so, he saw his reflection. He was not an ugly duckling anymore — he too was a swan!

The three other swans paddled right up to him and made him welcome. On the shore of the lake, a group of children cried out, "Look, a new swan has come, a new swan has come!" As she stared with wide eyes at the graceful birds, one little girl cried, "Yes, and the new one is the most beautiful of them all." And so he was.

Goldilocks and the Three Bears

This is a story about a little girl called Goldilocks
and a family of bears.

One morning, Goldilocks was out exploring when she came across
a house that she had never seen before. "I wonder who lives there,"
she thought. The front door was wide open, so she decided to go
inside and see if there was anyone at home.

"Hello!" called Goldilocks, but there was no answer. She tiptoed
into the kitchen and saw three bowls of porridge laid out on the
table. There was one big bowl, one medium bowl and one small
bowl. "Mmmm!" thought Goldilocks. "How delicious!" First, she
tasted the porridge in the big bowl, but that was much too hot.
Then she tasted the porridge in the second bowl, but that was
much too cold. Last, she tasted the porridge in the third bowl.
That was just right, so she ate it all up.

48

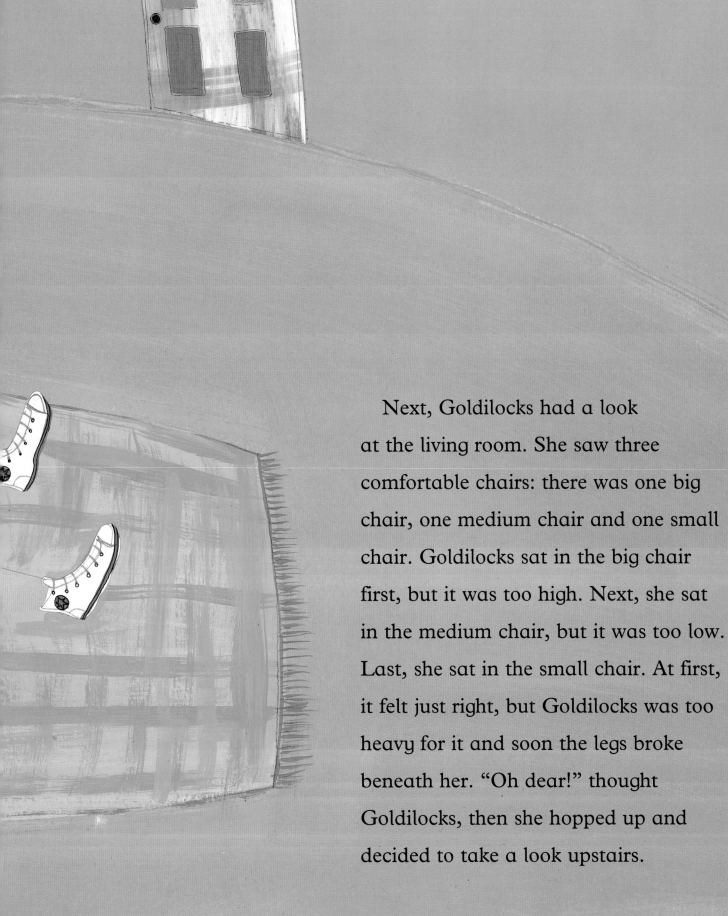

Next, Goldilocks had a look at the living room. She saw three comfortable chairs: there was one big chair, one medium chair and one small chair. Goldilocks sat in the big chair first, but it was too high. Next, she sat in the medium chair, but it was too low. Last, she sat in the small chair. At first, it felt just right, but Goldilocks was too heavy for it and soon the legs broke beneath her. "Oh dear!" thought Goldilocks, then she hopped up and decided to take a look upstairs.

At the top of the stairs, Goldilocks found a big bedroom. In the bedroom there were three beds: there was one big bed, one medium bed and one small bed. First of all, Goldilocks lay down in the big bed, but it was too hard. Then she lay down in the medium bed, but it was too soft. Last, she lay down in the small bed. It was perfect for her! Goldilocks curled up under the blankets and soon she was fast asleep.

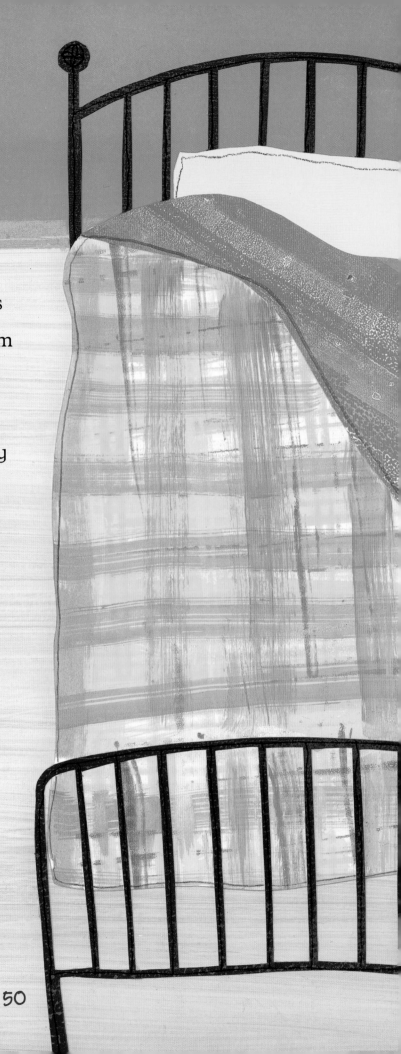

Now, this little house belonged to a family of bears, and just as Goldilocks was falling asleep, they came back for their breakfast. Right away, they knew that something was wrong.

"Someone's taken a spoonful of my porridge!" roared the father bear.

"Someone's taken a spoonful of mine, too!" exclaimed the mother bear.

And the baby bear cried, "Someone's taken more than a spoonful of my porridge — they've eaten it all up!"

The three bears went into the living room.

"Someone's been sitting in my chair!" roared the father bear.

"Someone's been sitting in my chair, too!" exclaimed the mother bear.

And the baby bear cried, "Someone's been sitting in my chair, and they've broken it into pieces!" Then he burst into tears.

The three bears climbed up the stairs to the bedroom.

"Someone's been sleeping in my bed!" roared the father bear.

"Someone's been sleeping in my bed, too!" exclaimed the mother bear.

And the baby bear cried, "Someone's been sleeping in my bed, and she's still here!"

Just at that moment, Goldilocks woke up. You can imagine what a fright she got when she saw three bears staring at her. She jumped right out of bed and ran down the stairs and out of the house and away through the woods until she was safely home again. After that, she took good care not to go inside other people's houses when she went exploring.

The Timid Hare

This is a story about a timid hare
and a wise lion.

The timid hare lived in a beautiful forest. His life was quiet and peaceful, but he couldn't help worrying. He worried about this and he worried about that, but most of all, he worried about what would happen to him if the earth fell apart.

One morning, the timid hare was lying in the sun. He was just beginning to relax when, as usual, he started to worry about the earth falling apart. Just at that moment, a fat mango fell from the tree behind him and broke open on the earth with a big splat!

Well, the timid hare jumped right out of his skin. "This is it!" he thought. "The earth is falling apart. I'd better get away!" And the timid hare ran as fast as he could. He didn't know where he was going, but he was so scared that he just kept on running.

Soon, another hare spotted him. "Whatever is the matter?" he called. The timid hare was almost too scared to stop, but he paused just for a second to shout, "The earth is falling apart!" Then he ran on, as fast as his legs could carry him.

"Help, help! The earth is falling apart!" cried the other hare, and soon every hare in the forest was on the run. Away they raced, through the trees and down to the riverbank.

A herd of deer was grazing quietly by the water. "Help, help!" cried the hares. "The earth is falling apart!"

58

"Oh no!" cried the deer, and they raced along with the hares.

Soon they came to a group of wild boars. "You're in a hurry!" said the boars. "Whatever's the matter?"

"The earth is falling apart!" panted the deer.

"Oh no!" cried the boars, and they joined the hares and the deer.

Soon they came to a group of buffaloes, wallowing in a waterhole. "What's going on? What are you all running from?" they called.

"Haven't you heard? The earth is falling apart!" cried the deer and the hares. And right away, the buffaloes joined them.

The animals raced toward a group of rhinos. When the rhinos heard what was happening, they joined the stampede too. Then the tigers heard, and they joined in as well.

The animals ran and ran until they reached the wide plain, where the lions lived.

Now, it so happened that one of the lions on the plain was very wise and very kind. When he saw all of the animals running toward him in a blind panic, he thought,

"I had better stop them, or they'll run all the way to the sea and drown."

So the lion dashed across the plain. He stopped in front of the racing animals and gave three enormous roars.

The animals slid to a halt. When they had quieted down, the lion asked, "What is the matter?"

"The earth is falling apart!" cried a rhino. And the animals were just about to start running again, when the lion asked a second question.

"And who has seen it falling apart?" he asked.

"Oh," said the rhino. "I'm not sure. I think it was the buffaloes."

The lion turned to the buffaloes. "Did you see the earth falling apart?" he asked them.

The buffaloes shook their horns. "No, we heard about it from the boars."

So the lion turned to the boars.

"We heard it from the deer," said the boars. And of course, the deer told the lion they had heard about it from the hares.

Finally, the timid little hare came forward.

"I heard the earth falling apart," he said in a small, timid voice.

"Did you, little one?" asked the lion. "And where were you when you heard this?"

"Well, I was resting under a mango tree in the forest . . ." the hare started.

"I think we had better go back to the mango tree and take a look," said the lion. "Jump on my back, and show me where you live. The other animals can wait here until we have got to the bottom of this."

So the timid hare sprang on to the lion's back. They raced across the plain, along the riverbank, into the forest and all the way to the mango tree.

When they got there, the lion saw right away that a fat mango had fallen to the ground earlier that day.

"Aha!" he said. "I think you must have heard that mango falling on the ground."

The timid hare hung his head and felt very embarrassed.

"Let's tell the others that there's nothing to worry about," said the lion.

So the timid hare climbed on to the lion's back once more and away they went, fast as the wind, back to the other animals, who were all anxiously waiting to hear their news.

"My friends," said the lion, "the hare did not hear the earth falling apart; he heard a fat mango falling on to the ground. There is nothing to worry about."

Then all of the animals turned back to their homes. After that, the timid little hare stopped worrying about the earth falling apart. He even learned how to lie quietly in the morning sun and relax every now and then.

The Three Little Pigs

This is a story about three little pigs and
a big, bad wolf.

The three little pigs were all pink and plump, and they all had curly whirly tails. When it was time for them to make their way in the world, their mother gave them a piece of advice. "Look after yourselves," she said, "and whatever you do, keep out of the way of the big, bad wolf." Then she gave each of them a good-bye nose rub, and off they went.

The first little pig scampered along until he came to a pile of straw.

"Aha!" thought the first little pig. "This straw is just what I need to build myself a cozy little house."

He set to work, and in no time at all his straw house was finished. He was just putting the finishing touches on it when who should come along but the big, bad wolf!

"Mmmm," said the big, bad wolf to himself. "That plump little pig would make a tasty mid-morning snack." And he licked his lips with his long, mean tongue. Then he walked right up to the little straw house, as bold as brass, and knocked on the door.

"Who's there?" called the first little pig, and his curly whirly tail gave a curly whirly tremble.

"It's only me, your friendly local wolf," his visitor replied. "Can I come in?"

But the first little pig remembered his mother's warning.

"No, no, no! Not by the hair on my chinny chin chin!"

"Then I'll huff and I'll puff and I'll blow your house in!" boomed the wolf.

And that was the end of the first little pig.

The second little pig scampered along until he came to a pile of sticks.

"Aha!" thought the second little pig. "These sticks are just what I need to build myself a cozy little house."

He set to work, and within a few hours his stick house was finished. He was just putting the finishing touches on it when who should come along but the big, bad wolf!

"Mmmm," said the big, bad wolf to himself. "Another plump little pig! Wouldn't he make a tasty lunchtime snack?" And he licked his lips with his long, mean tongue. Then he strode up to the little stick house, as bold as brass, and knocked on the door.

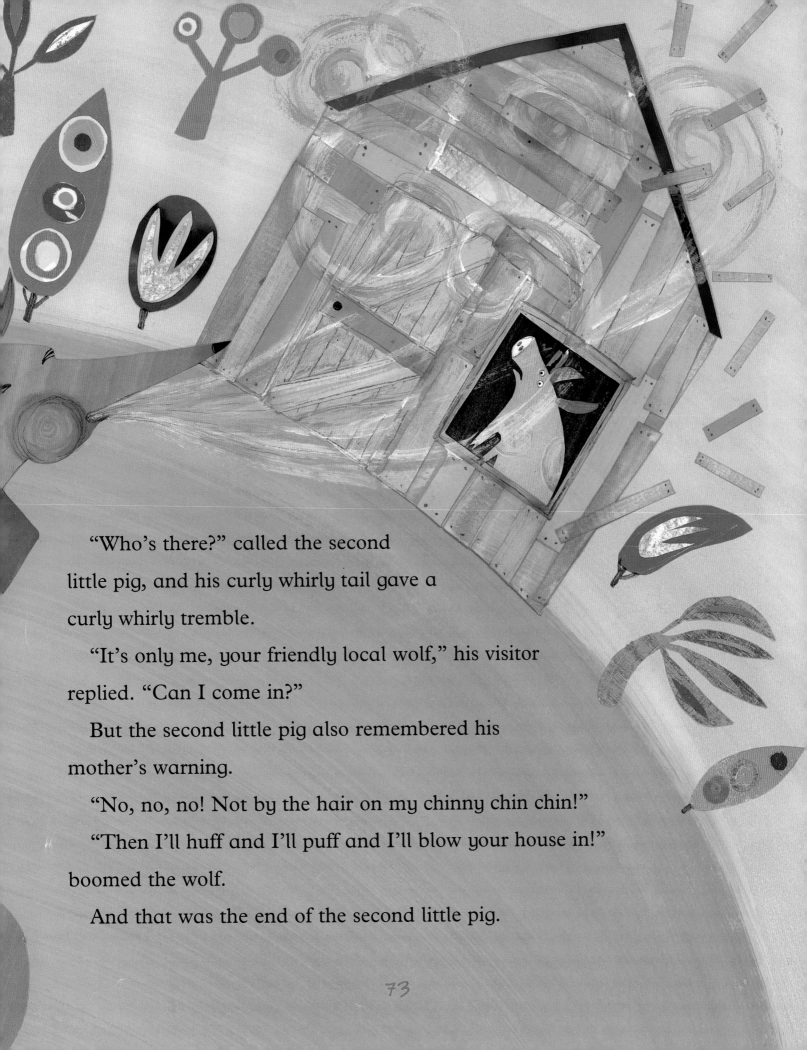

"Who's there?" called the second
little pig, and his curly whirly tail gave a
curly whirly tremble.

"It's only me, your friendly local wolf," his visitor
replied. "Can I come in?"

But the second little pig also remembered his
mother's warning.

"No, no, no! Not by the hair on my chinny chin chin!"

"Then I'll huff and I'll puff and I'll blow your house in!"
boomed the wolf.

And that was the end of the second little pig.

You are probably beginning to wonder what the third little pig was up to. Well, he didn't scamper off quite as quickly as his brothers. In fact, he sauntered along quite slowly, picking up a useful thing here, and a useful thing there. By the end of the morning, he had found a stack of bricks, a stack of roof tiles, some planks of wood, a box of tools and a big, red cooking pot.

The third little pig sat down for a while and made a plan. Then he set to work.

First, he dug a foundation for his house. Next he laid the bricks. Then he sawed up the planks of wood to make a door, and windows with shutters, and rafters for the roof. Finally, he laid the roof tiles.

The third little pig stepped back to check his work.

"Not bad," he thought to himself. "But I'm hungry! I'll put the pot on the fire and make some supper."

Soon a long plume of smoke could be seen rising from the house of the third little pig.

And soon the big, bad wolf — who, as you have probably guessed, was not very far away — sniffed the cool evening air and licked his lips with his long, mean tongue.

"Mmmm," the wolf said to himself. "This must be my lucky day. Yet another plump little pig waiting for a visit from his friendly local wolf! I think it's time for a little early-evening snack . . ."

And the big, bad wolf came striding up to the door of the little brick house and called out:

"Little pig, little pig, may I come in?"

But the third little pig's curly whirly tail went completely straight with alarm and he knew at once that whoever was at the other side of the door meant trouble.

"No, you may not!" he said.

"Then I'll huff and I'll puff and I'll blow your house in!" boomed the big, bad wolf.

And the big, bad wolf huffed and puffed and blew as hard as he could. But nothing happened. He could not blow the brick house down. In fact, he could not even budge a single brick.

Well, the wolf was furious, but he was not going to give up that easily. He stepped back a few paces and then ran at the little brick house, as fast as his legs would carry him. Just before he reached it, he hurled himself at the roof, but he lost his foothold and fell off backward, flat on the ground.

Inside the little brick house, the third little pig put a big pot of water on the fire, whistling merrily as he worked. Of course, this made the wolf even angrier. He took a few more paces back and then took another flying leap at the roof of the house, but his claws slipped on the shiny new tiles and this time he tumbled head first onto the ground.

Inside, the third little pig whistled merrily as the pot of water started to bubble and boil.

By now, the wolf was in a towering rage, but he had to wait a bit to get his breath back. When he had recovered, he charged at the little brick house and leaped toward the roof. This time he made it. He gave a roar of triumph, then he plunged down the chimney and fell right into the cooking pot! And that was the end of the big, bad wolf.

The next day, the third little pig put up a sign,
which said:

PIGS ARE WELCOME.
WOLVES ARE NOT.
VISITING WOLVES
WILL BE PUT IN THE POT.

The third little pig had a long and happy life,
and he was never troubled by wolves again.

Stone Soup

This is a story about a big, brown wolf on a dark and snowy winter night.

It was freezing cold that night and all the animals in the village were indoors, trying to keep warm by their fires. The wolf walked alone, carrying a big sack on his back. The first house he came to was the hen's house.

"Rat-a-tat-tat!" The wolf knocked on the door.

"Who's there?" asked the hen.

And the wolf answered, "It's me, the wolf."

The hen was very alarmed. "The wolf!"

"There's nothing to be afraid of," said the wolf. "I'm very old, and all my teeth have fallen out, so I couldn't eat you, even if I wanted to. Just let me in so that I can warm myself by your fire, and make us both a nice bowl of stone soup."

The hen was not at all sure what she should do. She wasn't quite convinced by the wolf's words, but she was curious too. She had never seen a real wolf; she had just heard stories about them, and for all she knew the stories could be nonsense. Besides, she rather wanted a bowl of hot soup. So she opened the door.

The wolf stepped inside. He gave a weary sigh as he laid his sack in front of the fire.

"Could you bring me your biggest cooking pot?" he asked.

"Er, I'm not sure," said the hen, feeling distinctly nervous. "Why do you need it?"

"Well, I can't make us some soup if I don't have a pot," said the wolf. "This is what I have to do. Here in my sack is a nice big stone. I just need to put it in a pot, and add some water, and wait."

The hen had never heard of such a thing.

"I always put some celery in when I make soup," she remarked.

"Mmm, we could add some of that as well," said the wolf.

So the hen went to fetch her cooking pot and the celery.

But the wolf's arrival hadn't gone unnoticed. The pig had seen him entering the hen's house and he was very worried about her, so he plucked up his courage and trotted across the street. "Rat-a-tat-tat!" The pig knocked on the door.

"Is everything all right?" he asked.

"Come in, come in," said the hen with a wave of her wing. "We're making stone soup."

"Stone soup? I've never heard of such a thing! Nothing but stone?"

"Well, I've suggested that we add some celery."

"Good idea," said the pig, "I'll bring along some zucchini."

So the pig trotted home to fetch his zucchini. When he came back, the duck and the donkey were at the door of the hen's house. They too had seen the wolf going inside and they too were very worried about the hen.

"Rat-a-tat-tat!" The donkey knocked on the door.

"Come in, come in," said the hen with a wave of her wing. "We're making stone soup."

The duck, who had done quite a bit of traveling in her time, said that she had had stone soup before, when she visited her relatives on the coast. "But they put leeks in it there," she added. So the hen turned to the wolf and asked if it was all right to add leeks.

"Of course, of course," murmured the wolf. So the duck and the donkey hurried home to fetch some leeks.

By now, the sheep and the goat were getting very alarmed, for they too had seen the wolf step inside the hen's house, and so far he had not stepped out. So they hurried over to her house and pushed open the door.

"What's going on in here?" they asked.

"I'm making stone soup with the wolf and the pig and the duck and the donkey," said the hen, who was now busy chopping up all the vegetables. "Would you like some?"

"Well, yes, but I think it would taste a lot better with a few carrots in it," said the goat. And the sheep added, "I think a turnip or two would make it much more tasty."

So they hurried home as well, and came back with a big basket of turnips and carrots.

As the soup started to simmer on the fire, the animals drew up benches and chairs and sat around in a circle. They swapped jokes and they shared stories and all of them had a grand old time.

"We should do this more often!" said the hen.

"I thought I was going to find chicken soup when I knocked on your door!" laughed the pig. Then he turned to the wolf. "You haven't told a story yet," he said.

But the wolf was quietly tasting the soup. "I think dinner is ready now," he announced.

The wolf served everyone and the meal went on for a long, long time. All of the animals had as much as they could eat. Then the wolf drew a long, sharp knife out of his sack. A tremble instantly ran around the group — perhaps the wolf was still hungry? Perhaps they were his next course?

The wolf looked up and smiled at everyone.
Then he bent over the cooking pot and gave the
stone a gentle poke with his knife.

"Ah!" he sighed. "The stone isn't ready yet. If
you don't mind, I'll put it back in my sack for
my supper tomorrow."

"Oh!" said the hen. "Are you leaving already?
We haven't heard your story yet."

"I'm afraid I have to go," the wolf replied.
"Thank you, though, for a very enjoyable
evening."

"Will we see you again soon?" asked the hen
as she showed him out. The wolf did not reply. I
wonder if he ever went back — what do you
think?

SOURCES

There's a theory that our professions as adults are often influenced by particular childhood experiences. This may be true in my case — one of my earliest memories is of sitting in an armchair as a young girl, reading a dog-eared edition of fairy tales illustrated by Arthur Rackham and passed down to me by my father. There were other versions of these stories in my parents' house too, as well as scratchy vinyl records in the nursery, so all of them are in my bloodstream. I have listed below the books that have informed *Storytime*:

The Cock, the Mouse and the Little Red Hen

The earliest version I know of this popular story is the one retold by Félicité Lefèvre, (E. Grant Richards, 1907). It appears in many other collections, including *Farmyard Tales from Far and Wide*, retold by Wendy Cooling (Barefoot Books Inc, Cambridge, 1998).

The Gingerbread Man

I grew up with the Ladybird version of this tale, and with burnt gingerbread biscuits from the Aga! It has been incomparably retold by storyteller Hugh Lupton (Barefoot Books Inc, Cambridge, 2003) who cites as his source Joseph Jacobs' *English Fairy Tales* (The Bodley Head, London, 1970).

The Ugly Duckling

My introduction to this story was through a song which, irritatingly, I can now only half remember. As an adult, I shared with my children the version retold by Jim Henson in *The Storyteller* (Boxtree, London, 1992). It is also beautifully translated by L.W. Kingsland in his *Fairy Tales from Andersen* (Oxford University Press, 1985).

Goldilocks and the Three Bears

This story comes to me from Flora Annie Steel's *English Fairy Tales* (Macmillan & Co., London, 1918). It was retold by Marleen Vermeulen in *Forest Tales from Far and Wide* (Barefoot Books Inc, Cambridge, 1998) and can also be found in countless picture book versions.

The Timid Hare

This folk tale about the absurd way in which rumors can escalate appears in many shapes and forms the world over. I know it from Flora Annie Steel's "Henny Penny" in her *English Fairy Tales* and from Noor Inayat Khan's *Jataka Tales*, illustrated by Willebeek Le Mair (George G. Harrap & Co. Ltd, London, 1939).

The Three Little Pigs

I have chosen to retell the shorter version of this classic folk tale, which also features in the nineteenth-century storyteller Joseph Jacobs' *English Fairy Tales* (see above), and was reprinted as a Puffin Classic. There are also numerous picture book versions, my favorite being Lane Smith and Jon Scieszka's *The True Story of the 3 Little Pigs* (Penguin Books, Inc, New York, 1996).

Stone Soup

This story crops up in many cultures, sometimes with a nail, sometimes with a stone, sometimes with another object as the main ingredient of the soup. The version I most admire is the French artist and writer Anaïs Vaugelade's retelling, *Une Soupe au Caillou* (Ecole des Loisirs, Paris, 2002).

Barefoot Books
Celebrating Art and Story

At Barefoot Books, we celebrate art and story with books that open the hearts and minds of children from all walks of life, inspiring them to read deeper, search further, and explore their own creative gifts. Taking our inspiration from many different cultures, we focus on themes that encourage independence of spirit, enthusiasm for learning, and acceptance of other traditions. Thoughtfully prepared by writers, artists and storytellers from all over the world, our products combine the best of the present with the best of the past to educate our children as the caretakers of tomorrow.

www.barefootbooks.com

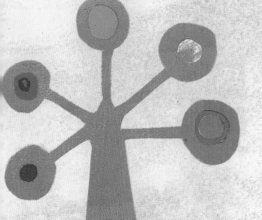